The Animals' Christmas Eve

By Gale Wiersum

Illustrated by Jim Robison

A GOLDEN BOOK • NEW YORK
Western Publishing Company, Inc., Racine, Wisconsin 53404

In the barn on Christmas Eve,
After all the people leave,
The animals, in voices low,
Remember Christmas long ago.

One small hen, upon her nest,
Softly clucks to all the rest:
"Little chicks, come, gather near.
A wondrous story you will hear."

Two white doves, on rafters high,
Coo a quiet lullaby:
"Long ago in manger hay,
The little baby Jesus lay.

"Three wise men from far away
Came to visit him one day,
For he was born," the doves recall,
"To be the greatest king of all!"

Four brown horses in their stalls,
Snug within the stable walls,
Tell of his birth: "'Twas long foretold
By chosen men in days of old."

Five gray donkeys speak with pride,
Remembering one who gave a ride:

"Our brother donkey went with them
From Nazareth to Bethlehem."

Six spotted calves now nibble hay
Like that on which the baby lay.

"They put him in a manger bed
So he could rest his sleepy head."

Seven goats, all black and white,
Describe the sky that holy night:

"A star appeared at early morn
To mark the place where he was born."

Eight nestling kittens lick their fur.
They nod their heads and softly purr:

"And he was wrapped in swaddling clothes
To keep him warm from head to toes."

Nine woolly sheep, down from the hill,
On Christmas Eve remember still:

"Shepherds heard the angels sing
Praises to the newborn king."

Ten soft lambs say Jesus' name.
"He was the Lamb of God who came.

He was the greatest gift of love,
Sent from his Father, God, above."

Eleven puppies listen well,
In hopes that they, in turn, can tell

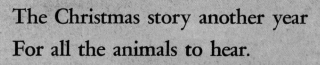

The Christmas story another year
For all the animals to hear.

Twelve chimes ring out from far away—
The lovely bells of Christmas Day.
And every beast bows low its head
For one small babe in a manger bed.